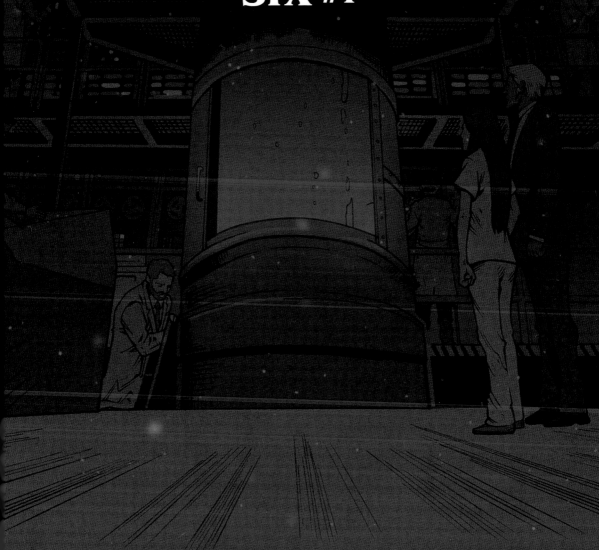

STRANGER THINGS

SIX #1

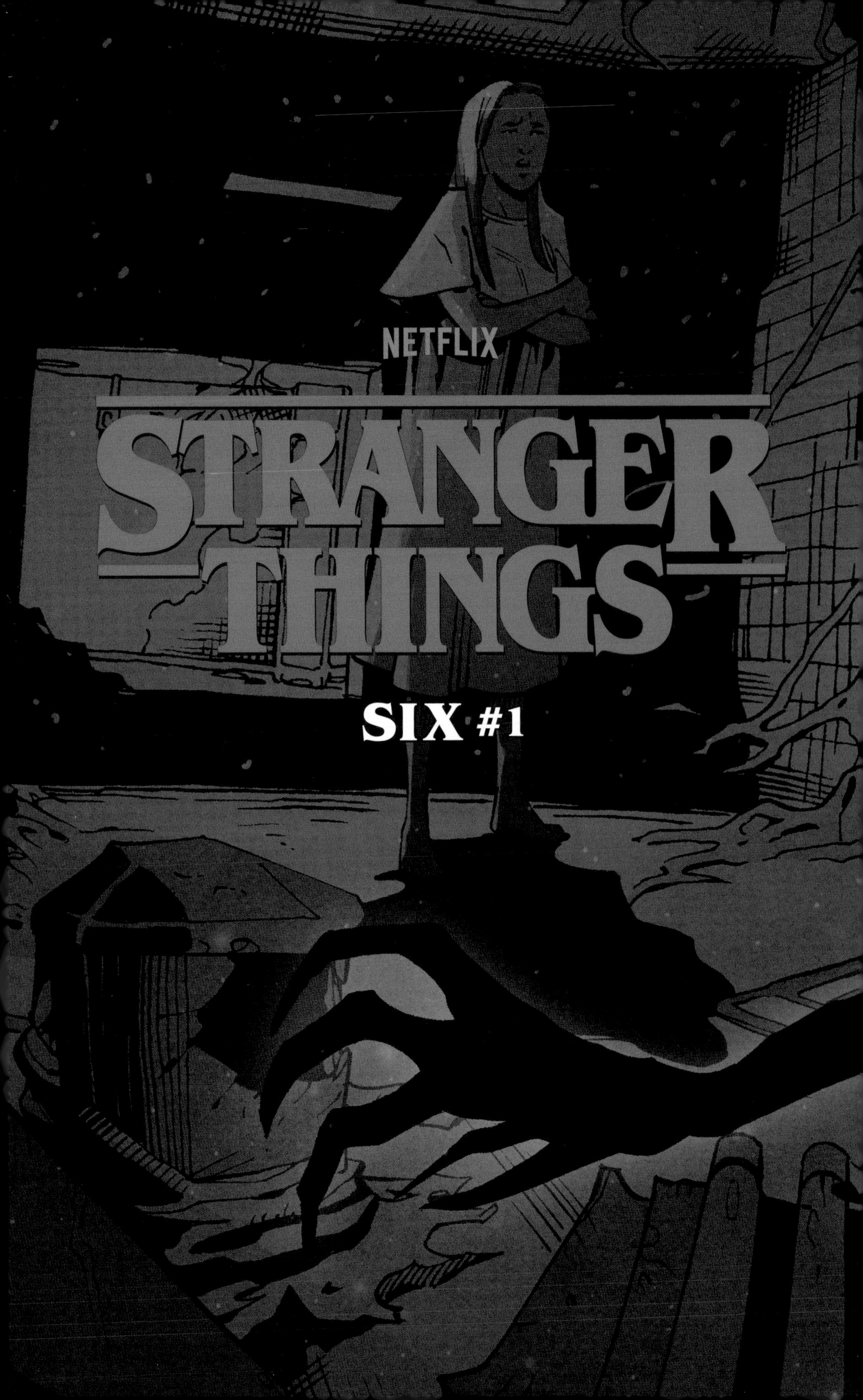
NETFLIX
STRANGER THINGS
SIX #1

script
JODY HOUSER

pencils
EDGAR SALAZAR

inks
KEITH CHAMPAGNE

colors
MARISSA LOUISE

lettering
NATE PIEKOS OF BLAMBOT®

front cover art by
KYLE LAMBERT

chapter break art by
ALEKSI BRICLOT

President and Publisher
MIKE RICHARDSON

Editor
SPENCER CUSHING

ABDO
Spotlight

DARK
HORSE
BOOKS

ABDOBOOKS.COM

Reinforced library bound edition published in 2020 by Spotlight, a division of ABDO, PO Box 398166, Minneapolis, Minnesota 55439. Spotlight produces high-quality reinforced library bound editions for schools and libraries.
Published by agreement with Dark Horse Comics.

Printed in the United States of America, North Mankato, Minnesota.
092019
012020

THIS BOOK CONTAINS
RECYCLED MATERIALS

Library of Congress Control Number: 2019942387

Publisher's Cataloging-in-Publication Data

Names: Houser, Jody, author. | Salazar, Edgar; Champagne, Keith; Louise, Marissa; Piekos, Nate, illustrators.
Title: Six / by Jody Houser; illustrated by Edgar Salazar; Keith Champagne; Marissa Louise; Nate Piekos.
Description: Minneapolis, Minnesota : Spotlight, 2020 | Series: Stranger things
Summary: A teenage girl with precognitive abilities ends up as the pawn of a government agency that wants to harness her powers for its own ends.
Identifiers: ISBN 9781532144400 (#1, lib. bdg.) | ISBN 9781532144417 (#2, lib. bdg.) | ISBN 9781532144424 (#3, lib. bdg.) | ISBN 9781532144431 (#4, lib. bdg.)
Subjects: LCSH: Stranger things (Television program)--Juvenile fiction. | Science fiction television programs--Juvenile fiction. | Supernatural disappearances--Juvenile fiction. | Monsters--Juvenile fiction. | Graphic novels--Juvenile fiction. | Comic books, strips, etc.--Juvenile fiction.
Classification: DDC 741.5--dc23

Spotlight

A Division of ABDO
abdobooks.com

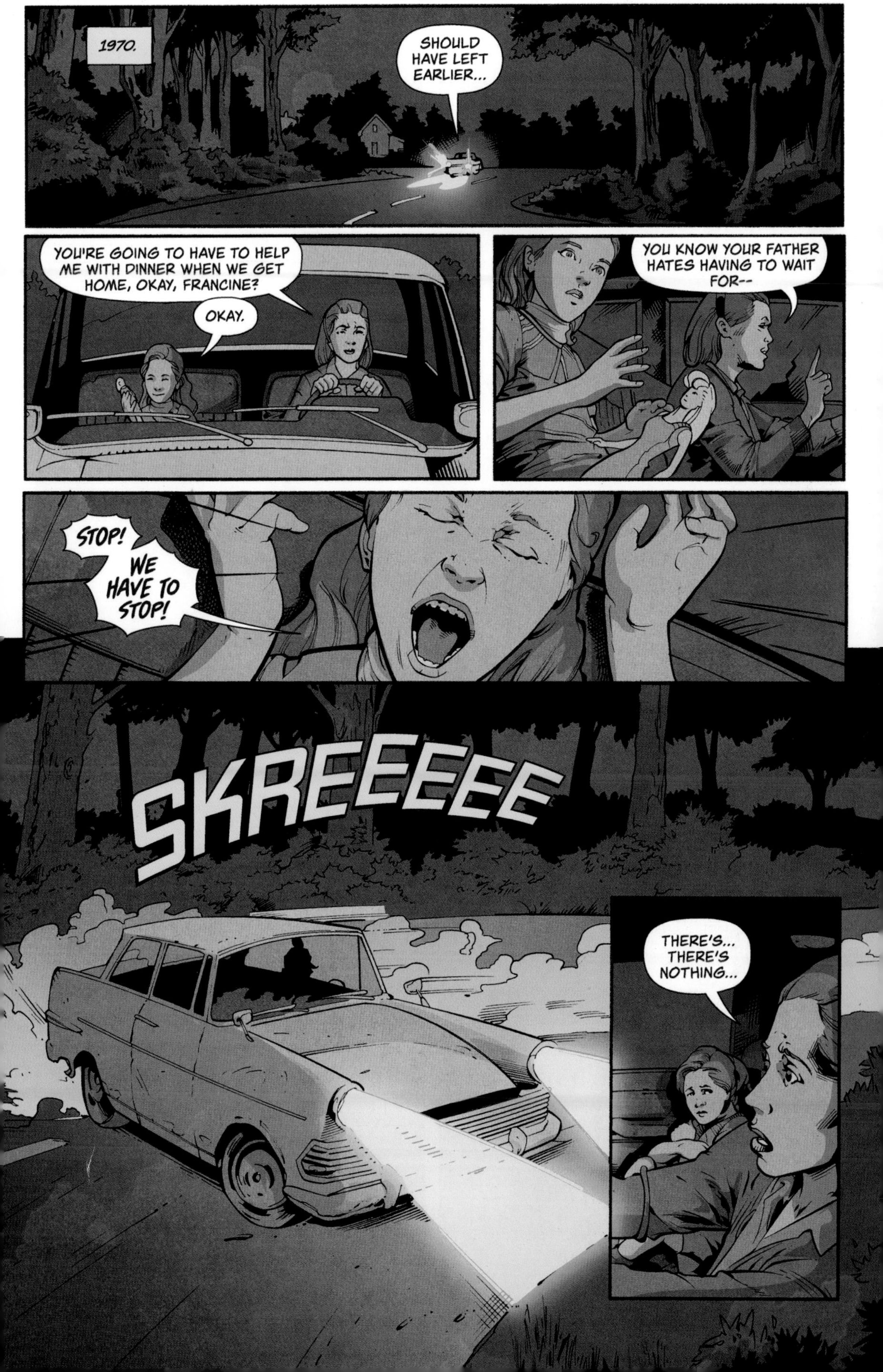
1970.
SHOULD HAVE LEFT EARLIER...
YOU'RE GOING TO HAVE TO HELP ME WITH DINNER WHEN WE GET HOME, OKAY, FRANCINE?
OKAY.
YOU KNOW YOUR FATHER HATES HAVING TO WAIT FOR--
STOP!
WE HAVE TO STOP!
SKREEEEE
THERE'S... THERE'S NOTHING...

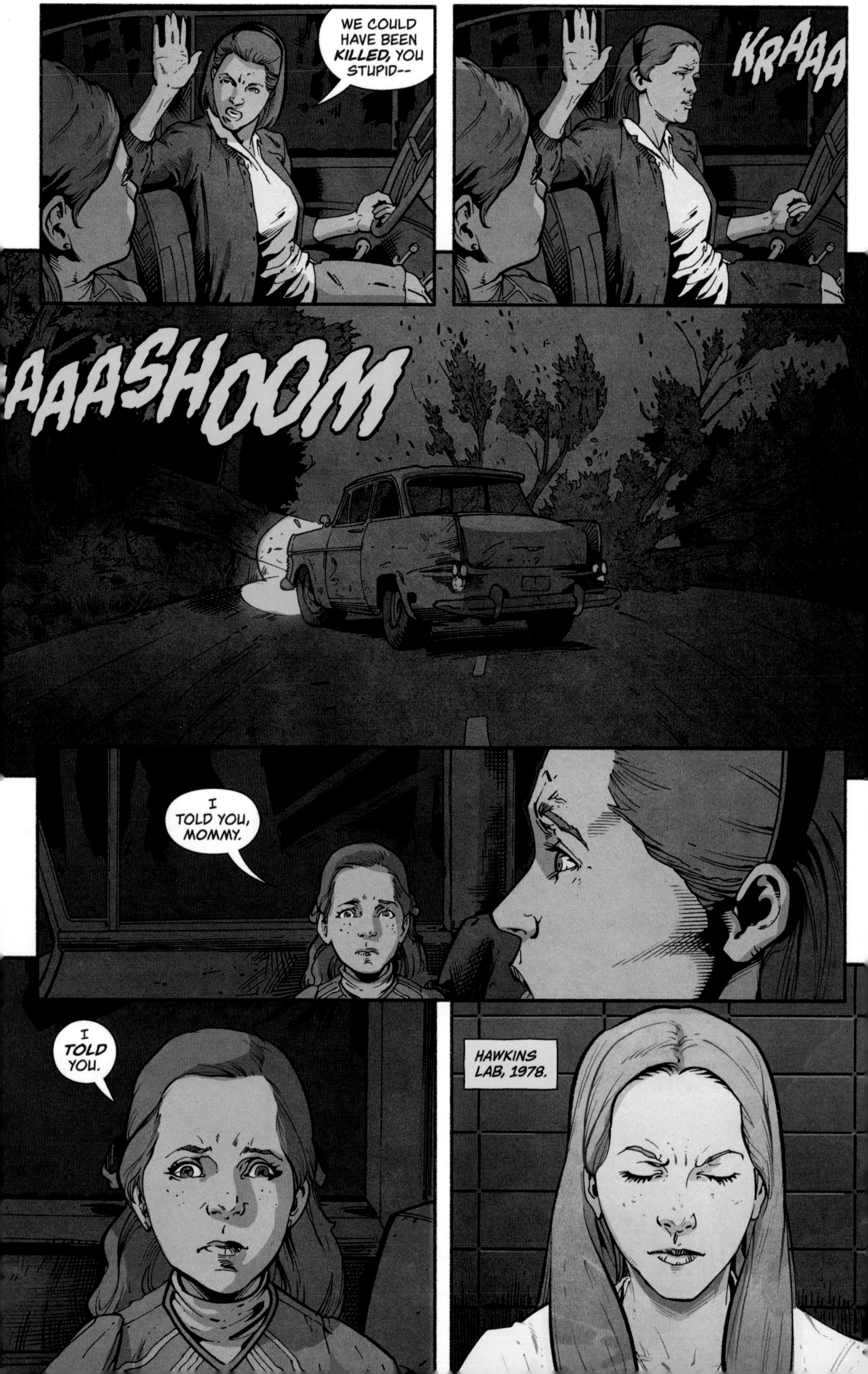
WE COULD HAVE BEEN KILLED, YOU STUPID--
KRAAAAASHOOM
I TOLD YOU, MOMMY.
I TOLD YOU.
HAWKINS LAB, 1978.

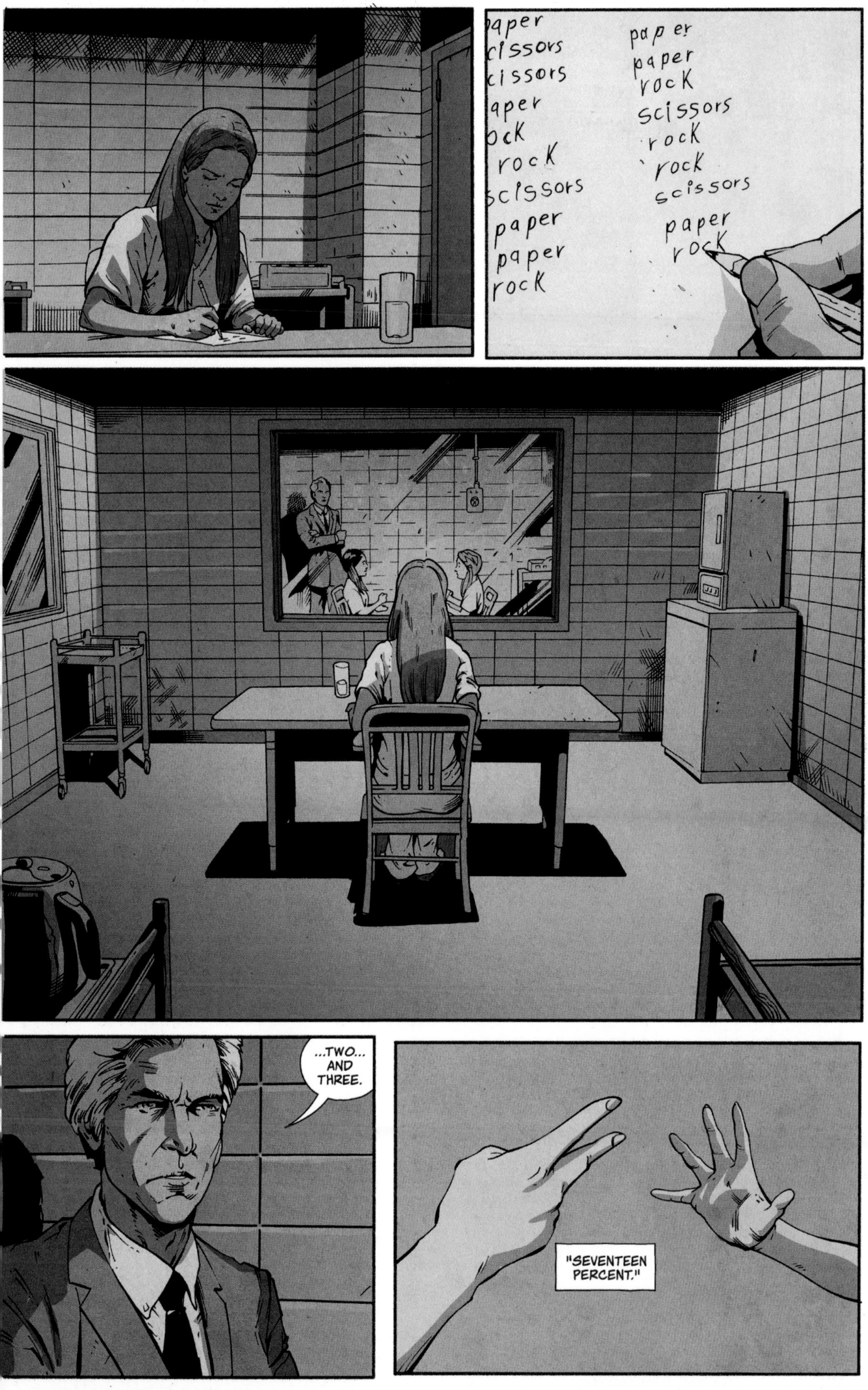

paper
scissors
rock
paper
paper
rock
scissors
rock
rock
scissors
paper
paper
rock
rock
scissors
paper
rock
...TWO... AND THREE.
"SEVENTEEN PERCENT."

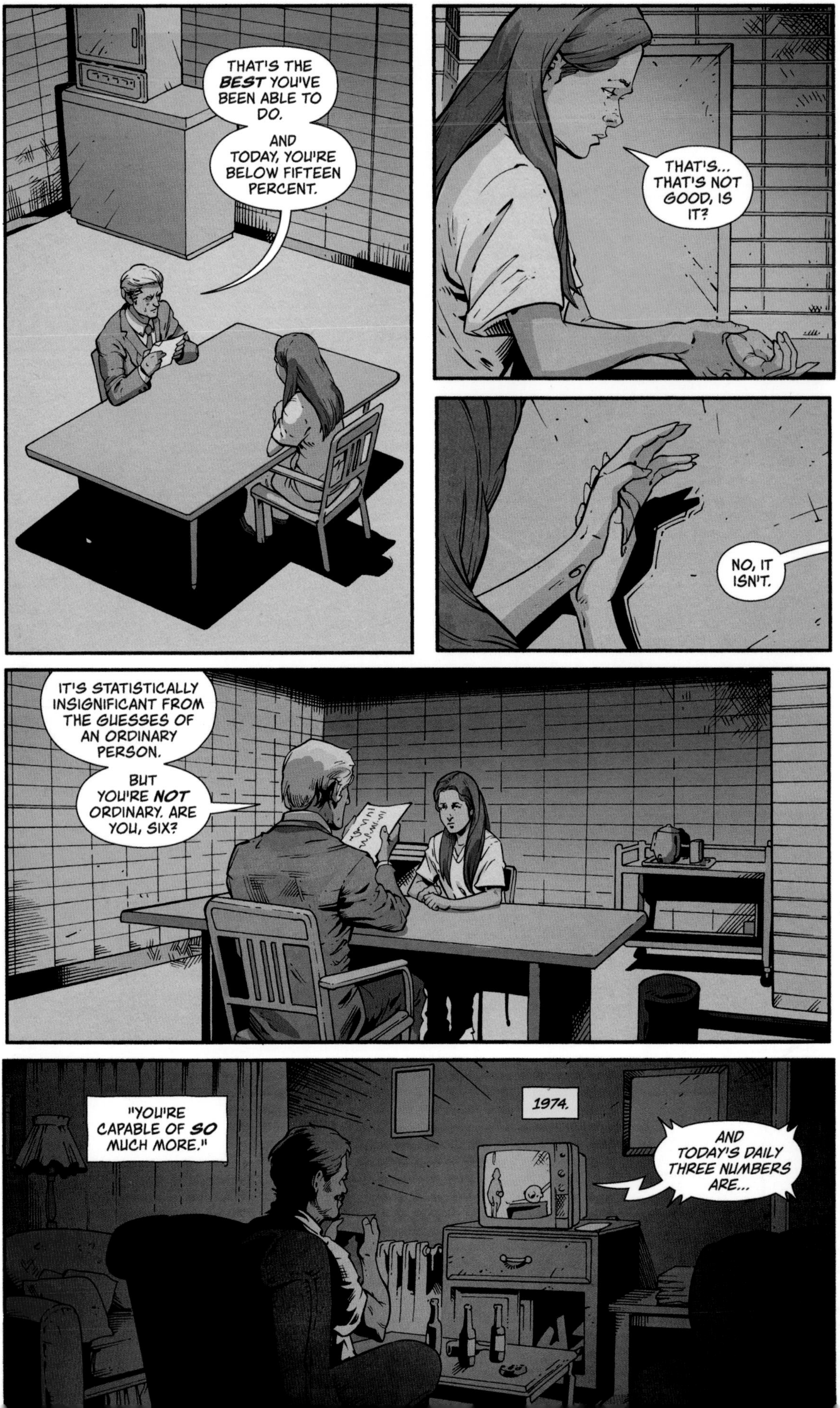
THAT'S THE BEST YOU'VE BEEN ABLE TO DO.
AND TODAY, YOU'RE BELOW FIFTEEN PERCENT.
THAT'S... THAT'S NOT GOOD, IS IT?
NO, IT ISN'T.
IT'S STATISTICALLY INSIGNIFICANT FROM THE GUESSES OF AN ORDINARY PERSON.
BUT YOU'RE NOT ORDINARY. ARE YOU, SIX?
"YOU'RE CAPABLE OF SO MUCH MORE."
1974.
AND TODAY'S DAILY THREE NUMBERS ARE...

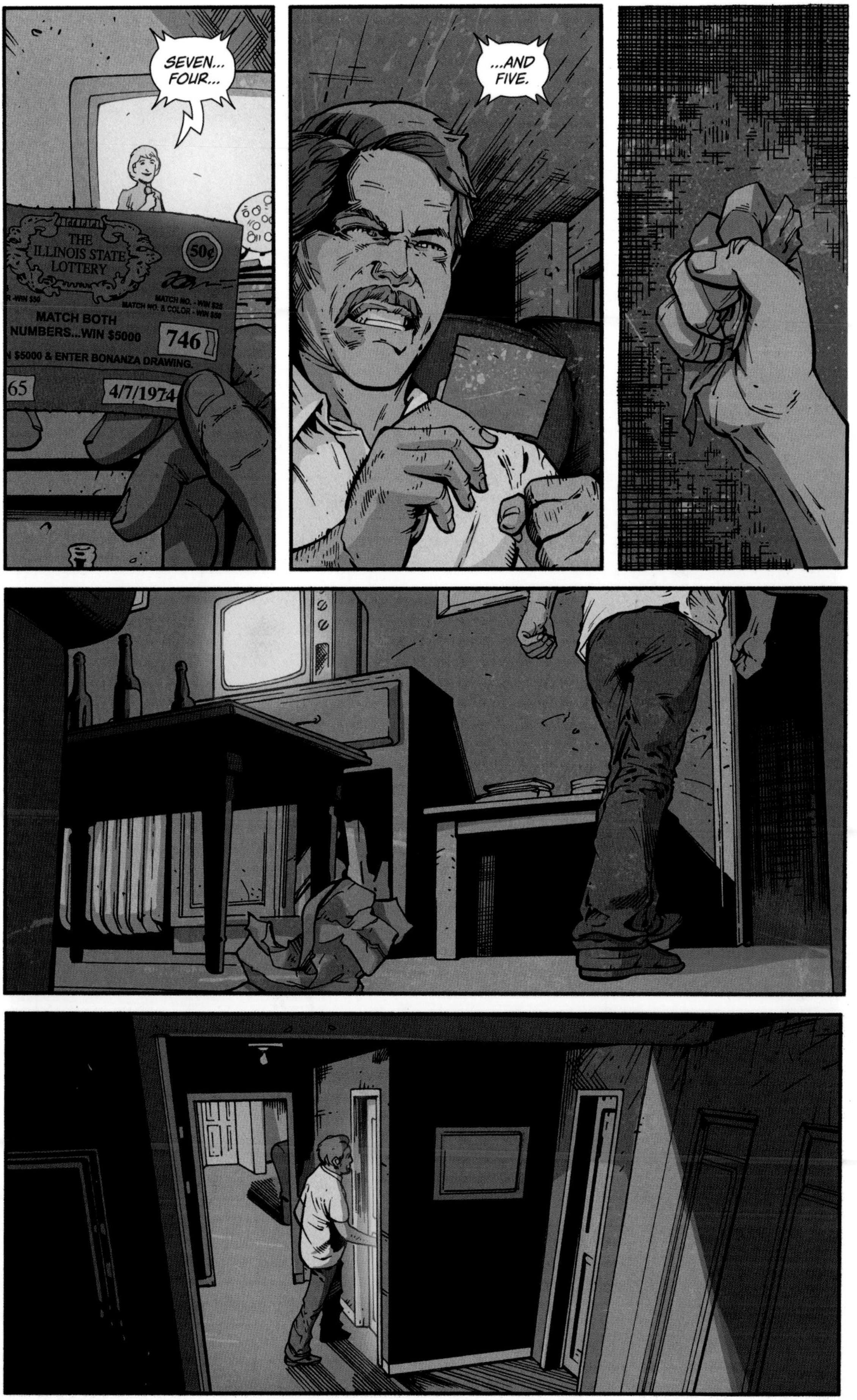
SEVEN... FOUR...
THE ILLINOIS STATE LOTTERY
50¢
MATCH NO. - WIN $25
MATCH NO. & COLOR - WIN $50
MATCH BOTH NUMBERS...WIN $5000
746
4/7/1974
...AND FIVE.

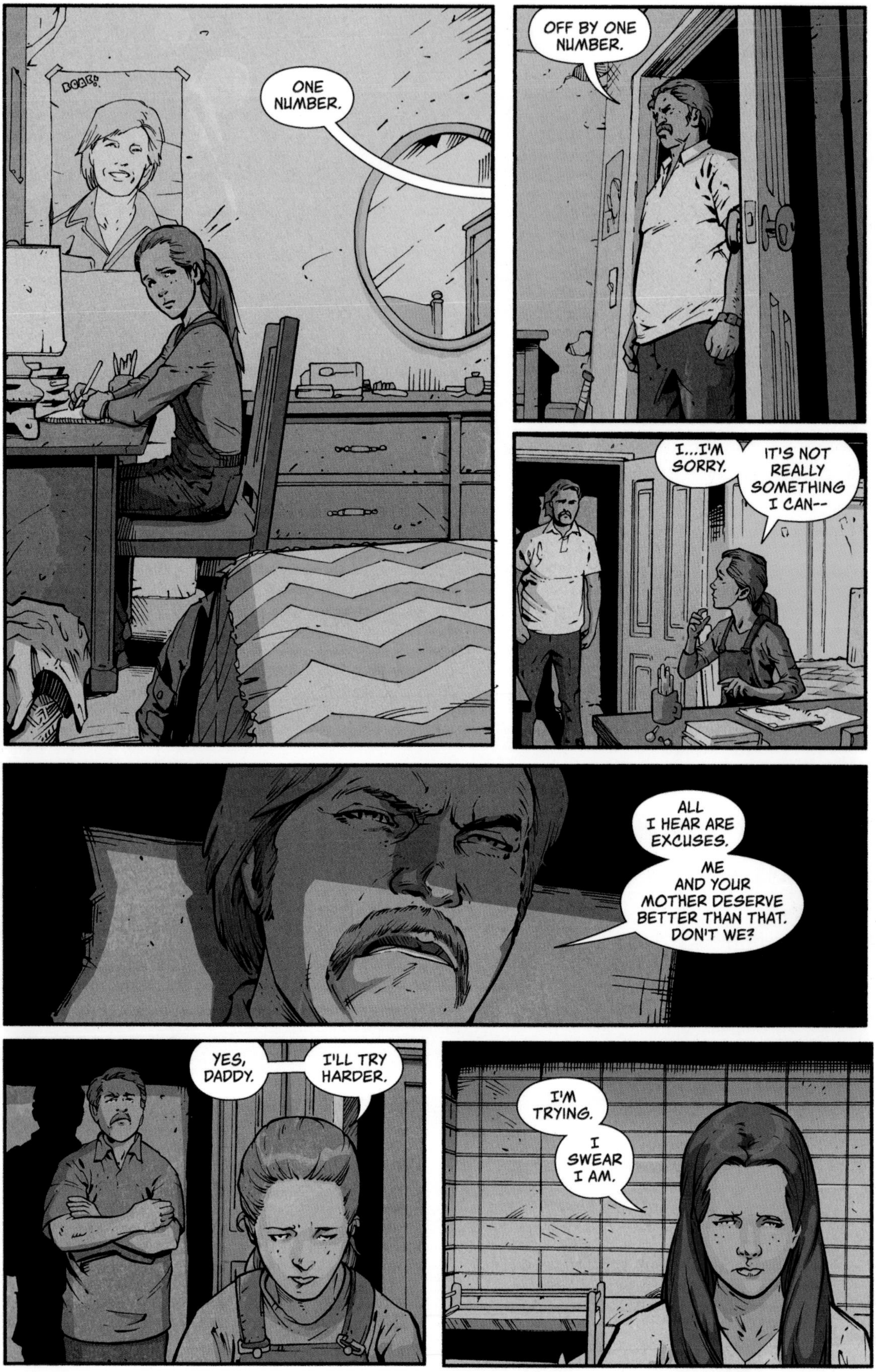
ROAR!
ONE NUMBER.
OFF BY ONE NUMBER.
I...I'M SORRY.
IT'S NOT REALLY SOMETHING I CAN--
ALL I HEAR ARE EXCUSES.
ME AND YOUR MOTHER DESERVE BETTER THAN THAT. DON'T WE?
YES, DADDY.
I'LL TRY HARDER.
I'M TRYING.
I SWEAR I AM.

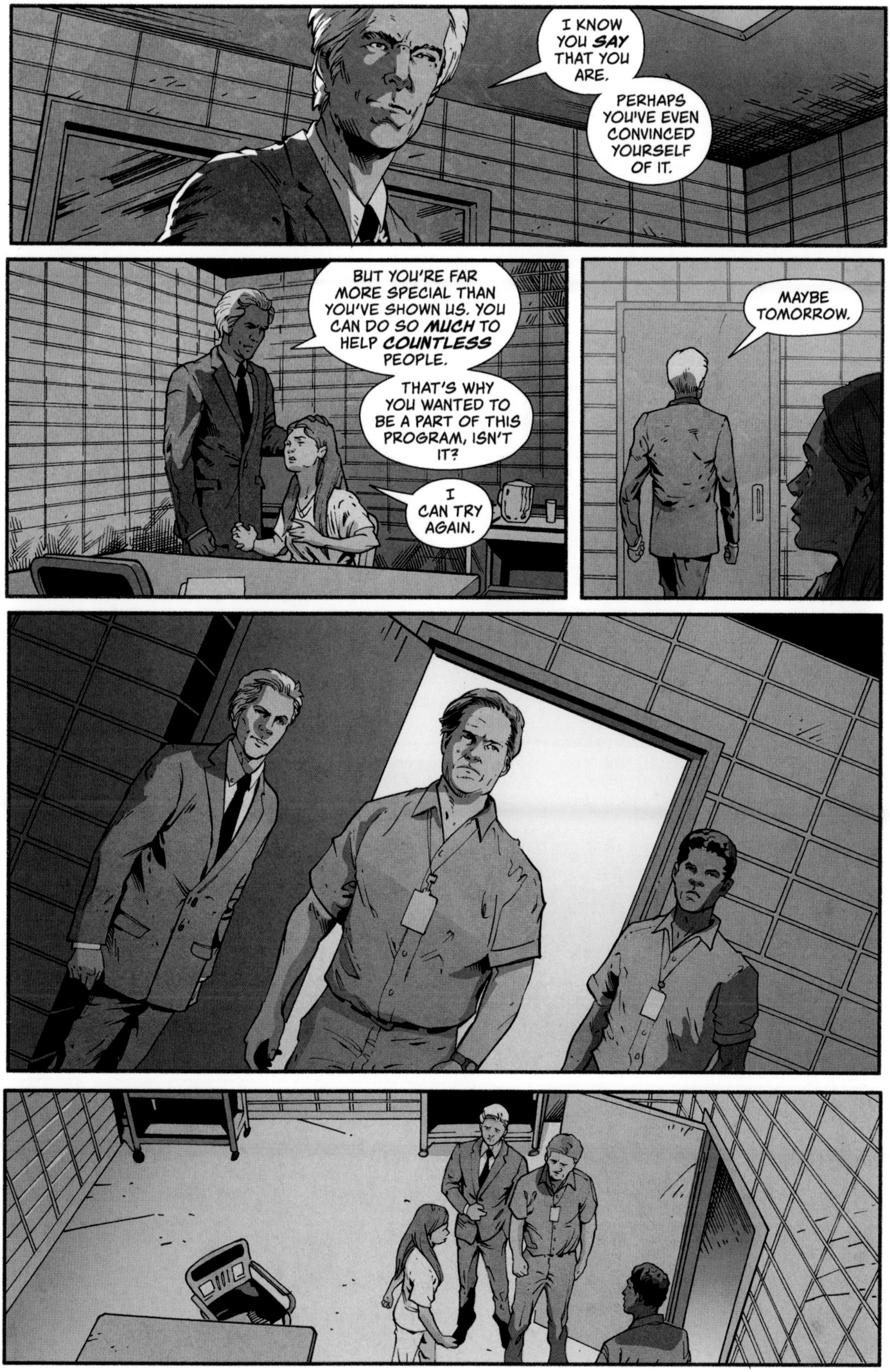
I KNOW YOU SAY THAT YOU ARE.
PERHAPS YOU'VE EVEN CONVINCED YOURSELF OF IT.
BUT YOU'RE FAR MORE SPECIAL THAN YOU'VE SHOWN US. YOU CAN DO SO MUCH TO HELP COUNTLESS PEOPLE.
THAT'S WHY YOU WANTED TO BE A PART OF THIS PROGRAM, ISN'T IT?
I CAN TRY AGAIN.
MAYBE TOMORROW.

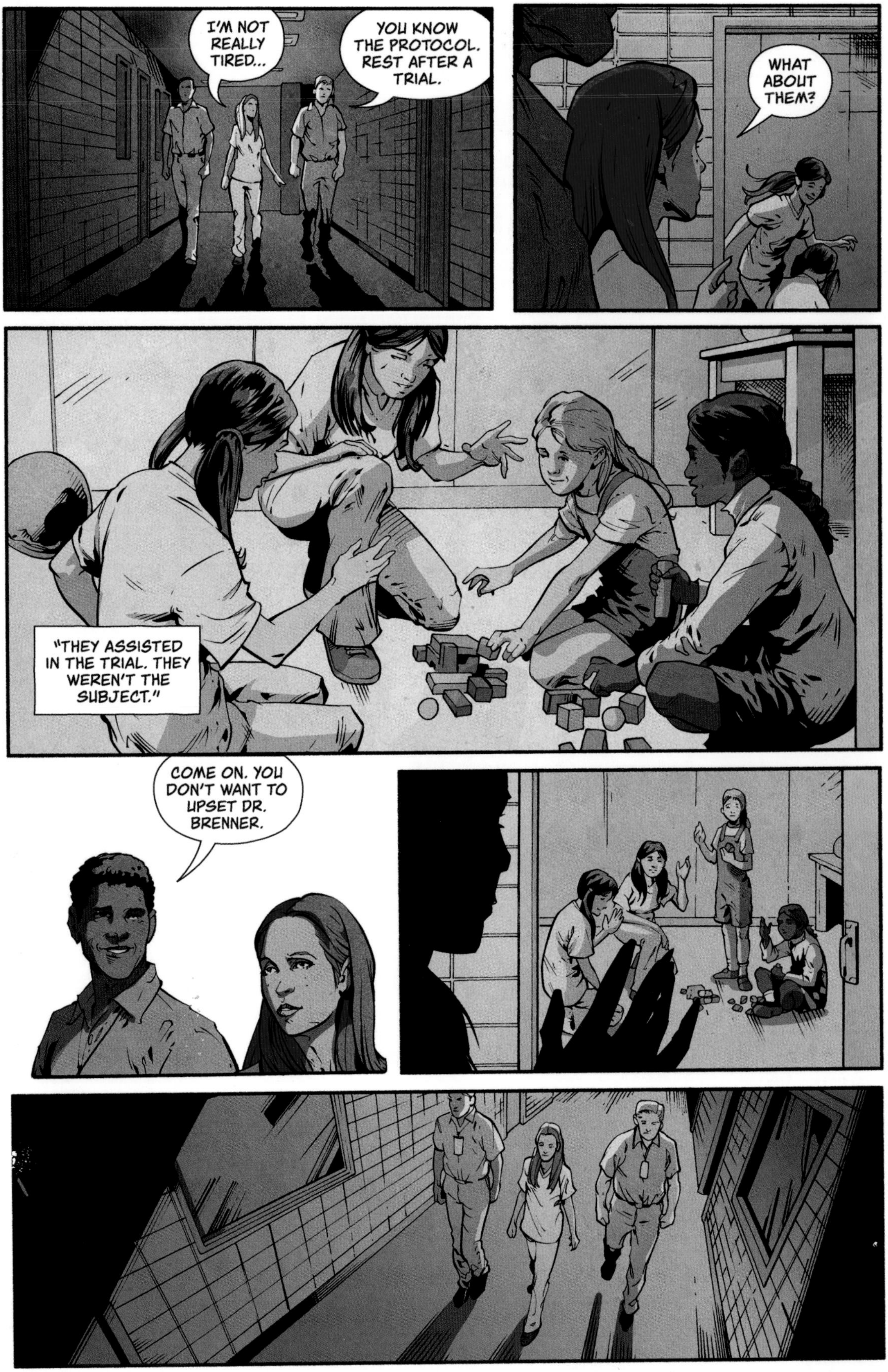
I'M NOT REALLY TIRED...
YOU KNOW THE PROTOCOL. REST AFTER A TRIAL.
WHAT ABOUT THEM?
"THEY ASSISTED IN THE TRIAL. THEY WEREN'T THE SUBJECT."
COME ON. YOU DON'T WANT TO UPSET DR. BRENNER.

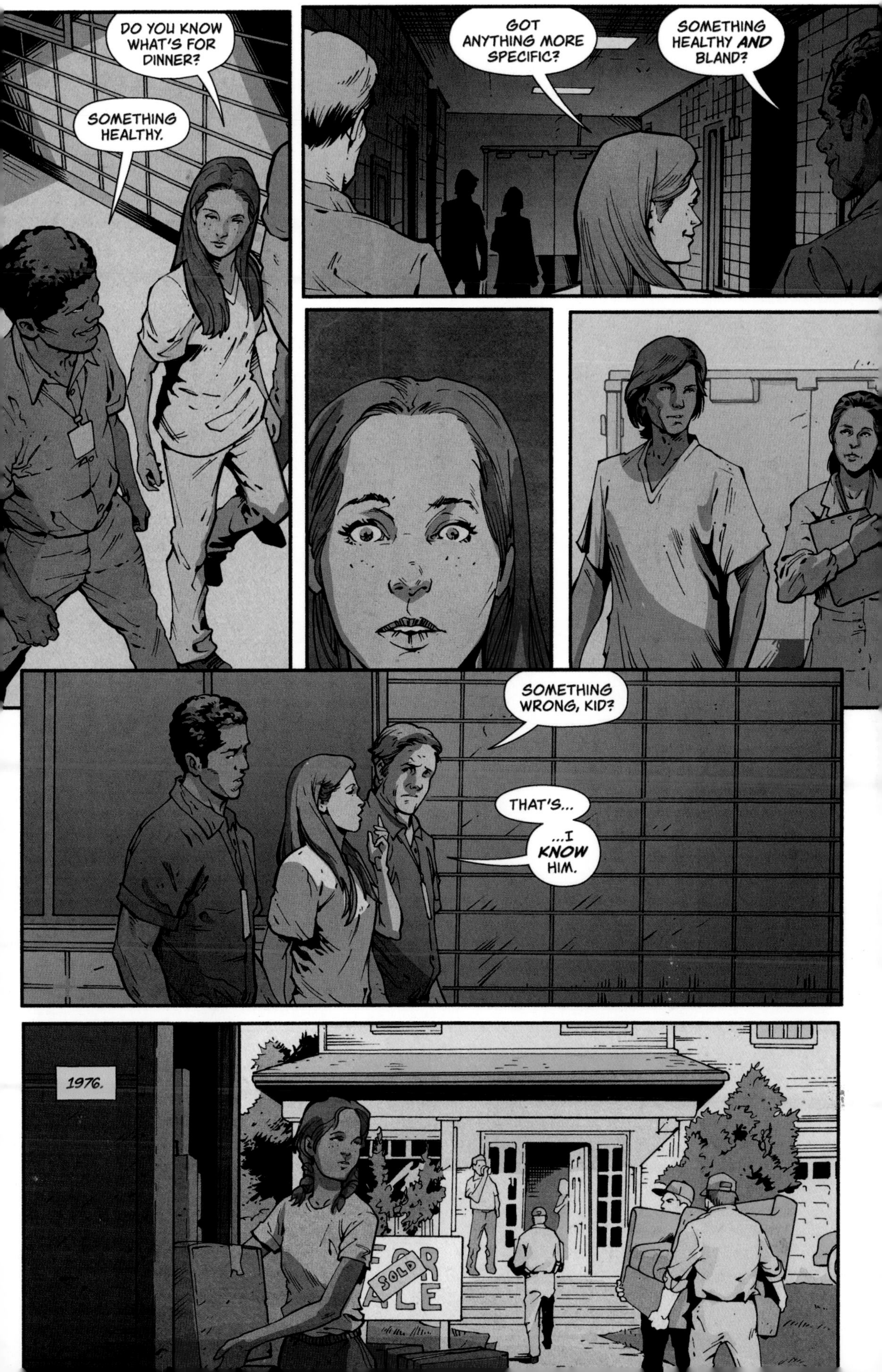
DO YOU KNOW WHAT'S FOR DINNER?
SOMETHING HEALTHY.
GOT ANYTHING MORE SPECIFIC?
SOMETHING HEALTHY **AND** BLAND?
SOMETHING WRONG, KID?
THAT'S...
...I **KNOW** HIM.
1976.
SOLD
FOR
ALE

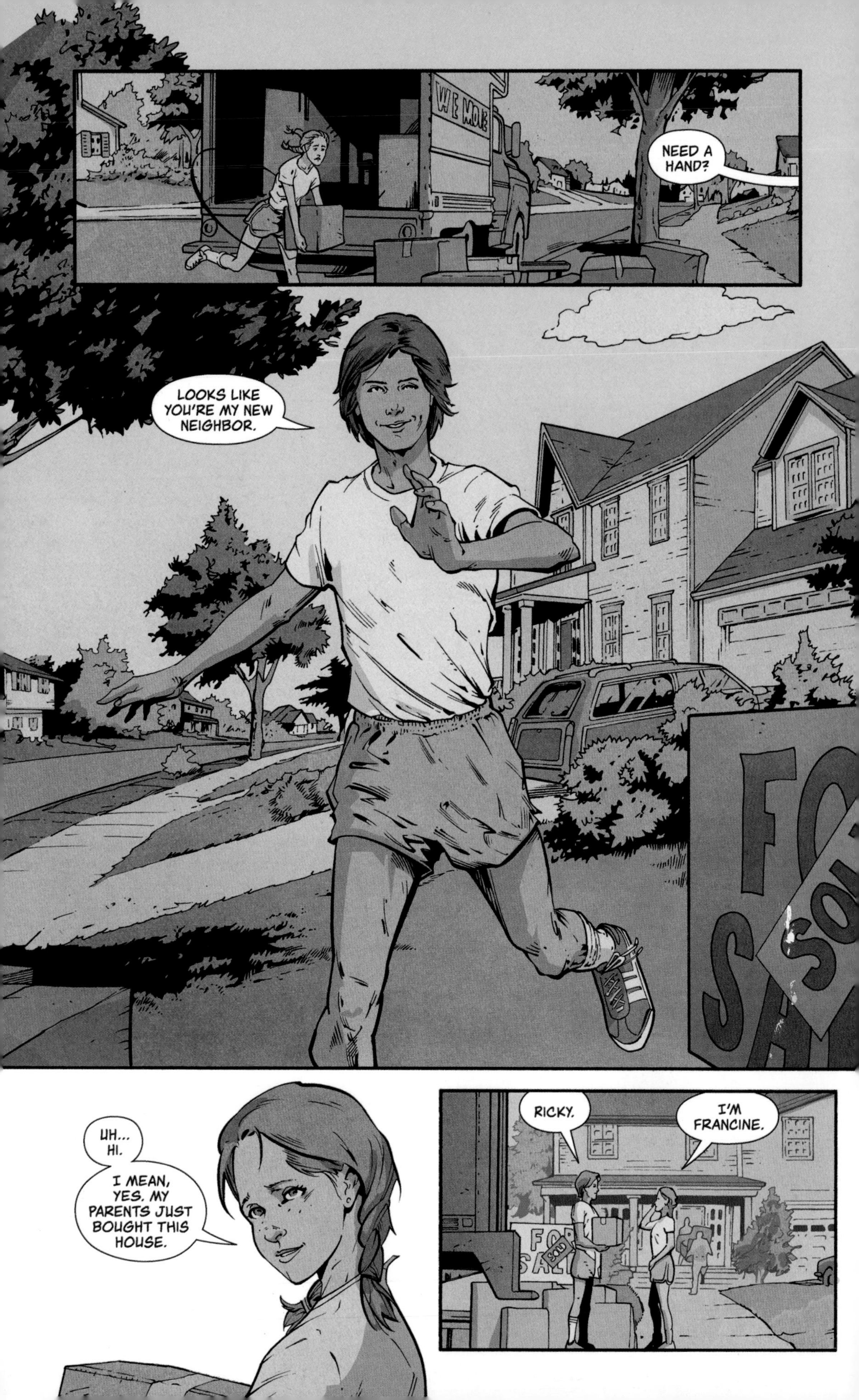
WE MOVE
NEED A HAND?
LOOKS LIKE YOU'RE MY NEW NEIGHBOR.
FOR SALE
SOLD
UH... HI.
I MEAN, YES. MY PARENTS JUST BOUGHT THIS HOUSE.
I'M FRANCINE.
RICKY.

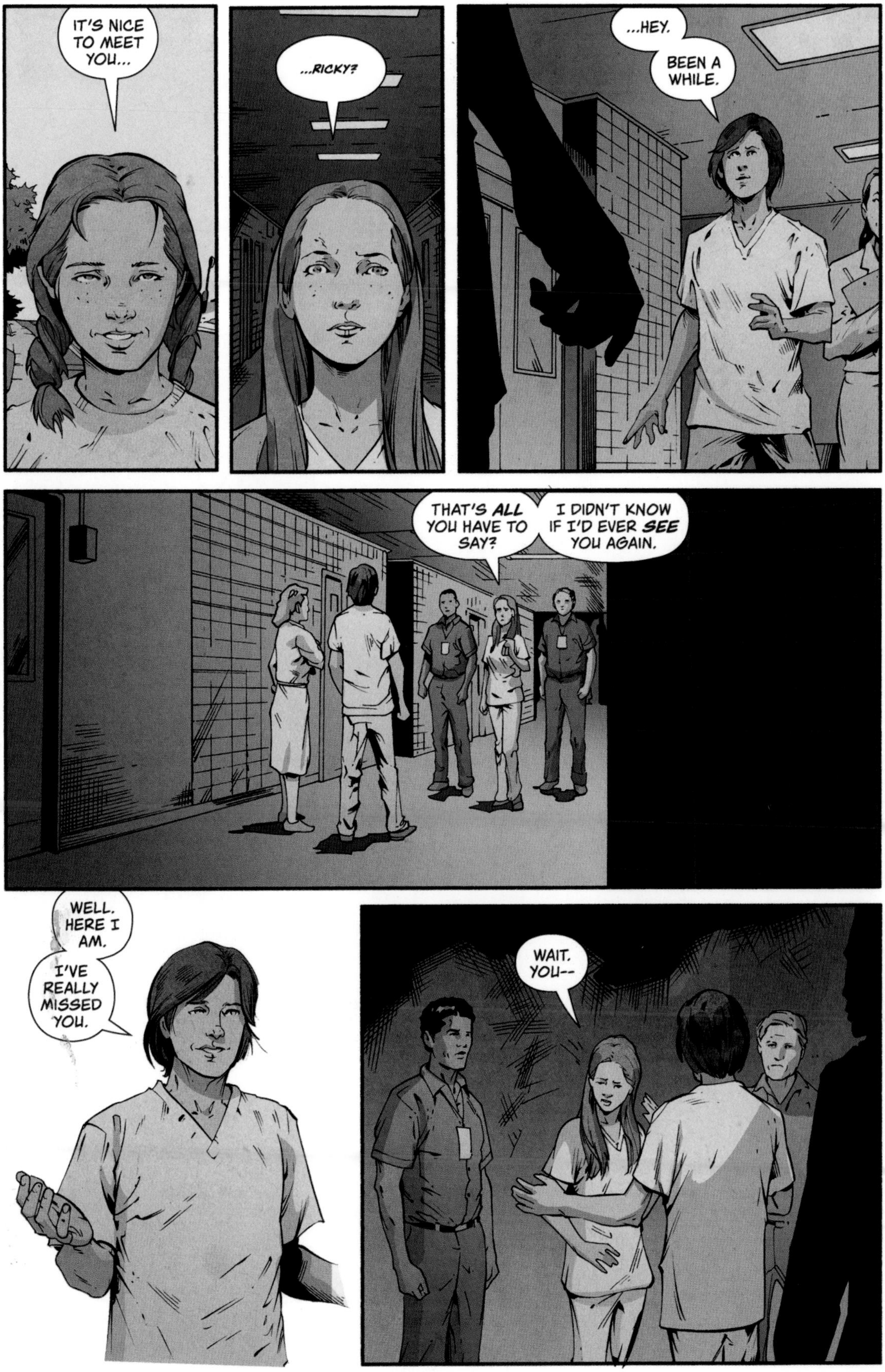
IT'S NICE TO MEET YOU...
...RICKY?
...HEY.
BEEN A WHILE.
THAT'S ALL YOU HAVE TO SAY?
I DIDN'T KNOW IF I'D EVER SEE YOU AGAIN.
WELL. HERE I AM.
I'VE REALLY MISSED YOU.
WAIT. YOU--

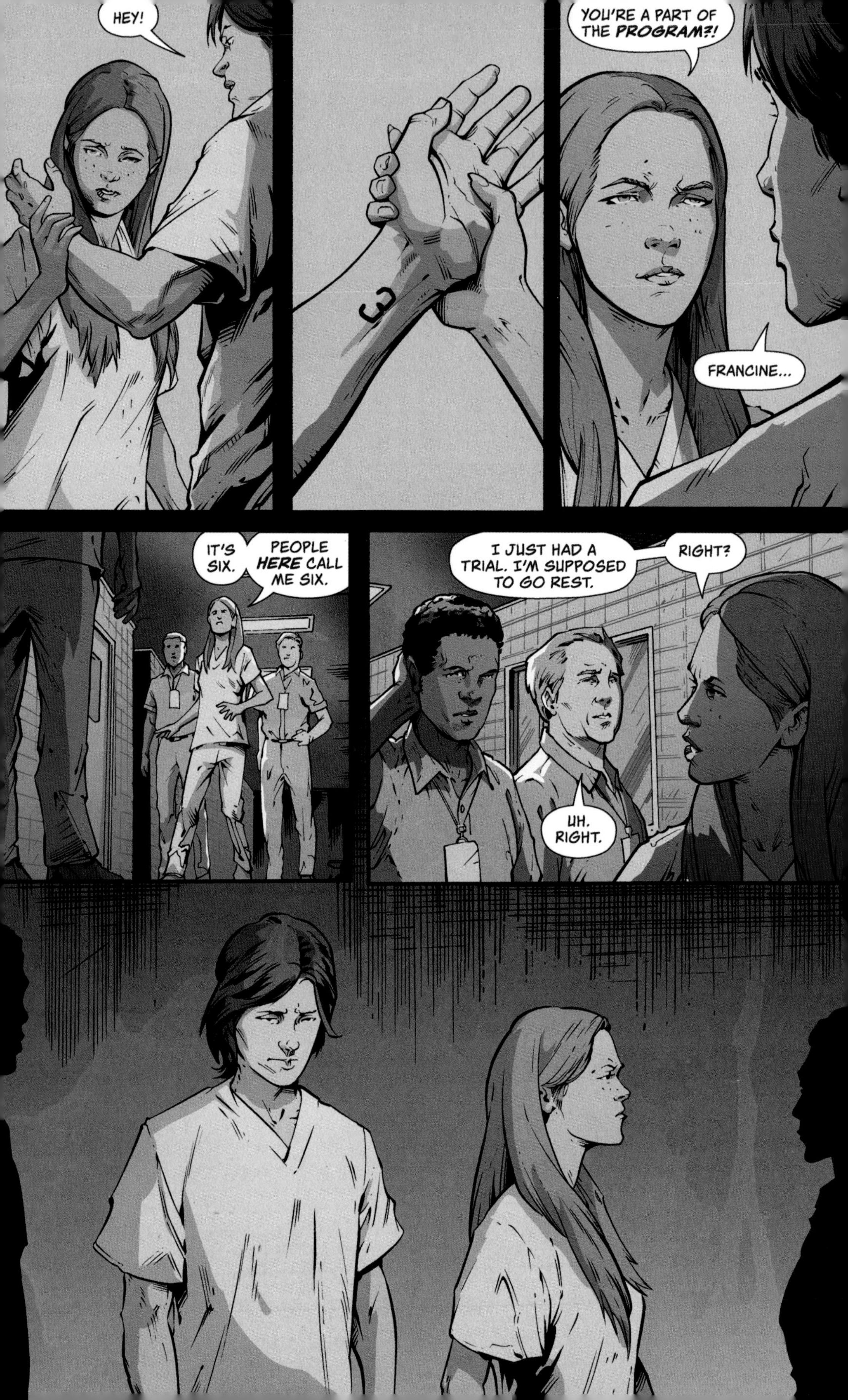
HEY!
YOU'RE A PART OF THE *PROGRAM*?!
FRANCINE...
IT'S SIX.
PEOPLE *HERE* CALL ME SIX.
I JUST HAD A TRIAL. I'M SUPPOSED TO GO REST.
RIGHT?
UH. RIGHT.

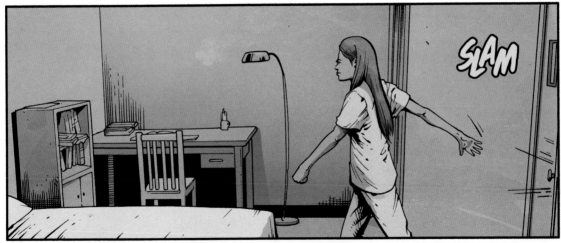

HEY. DO YOU, UH--

I'D LIKE TO BE ALONE, PLEASE.

klik

DANG IT, RICKY...

THAP

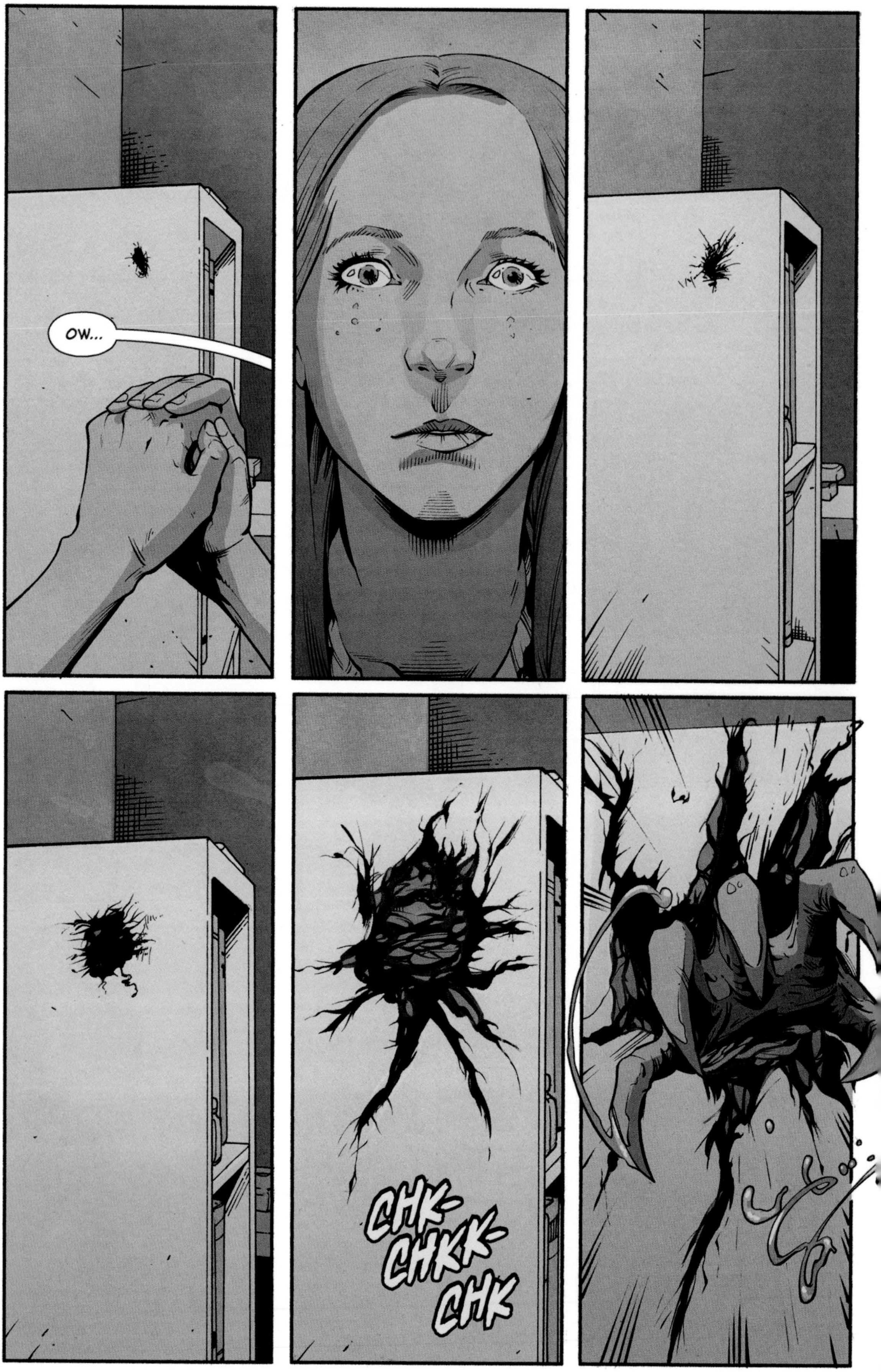
OW...
CHK-
CHKK-
CHK

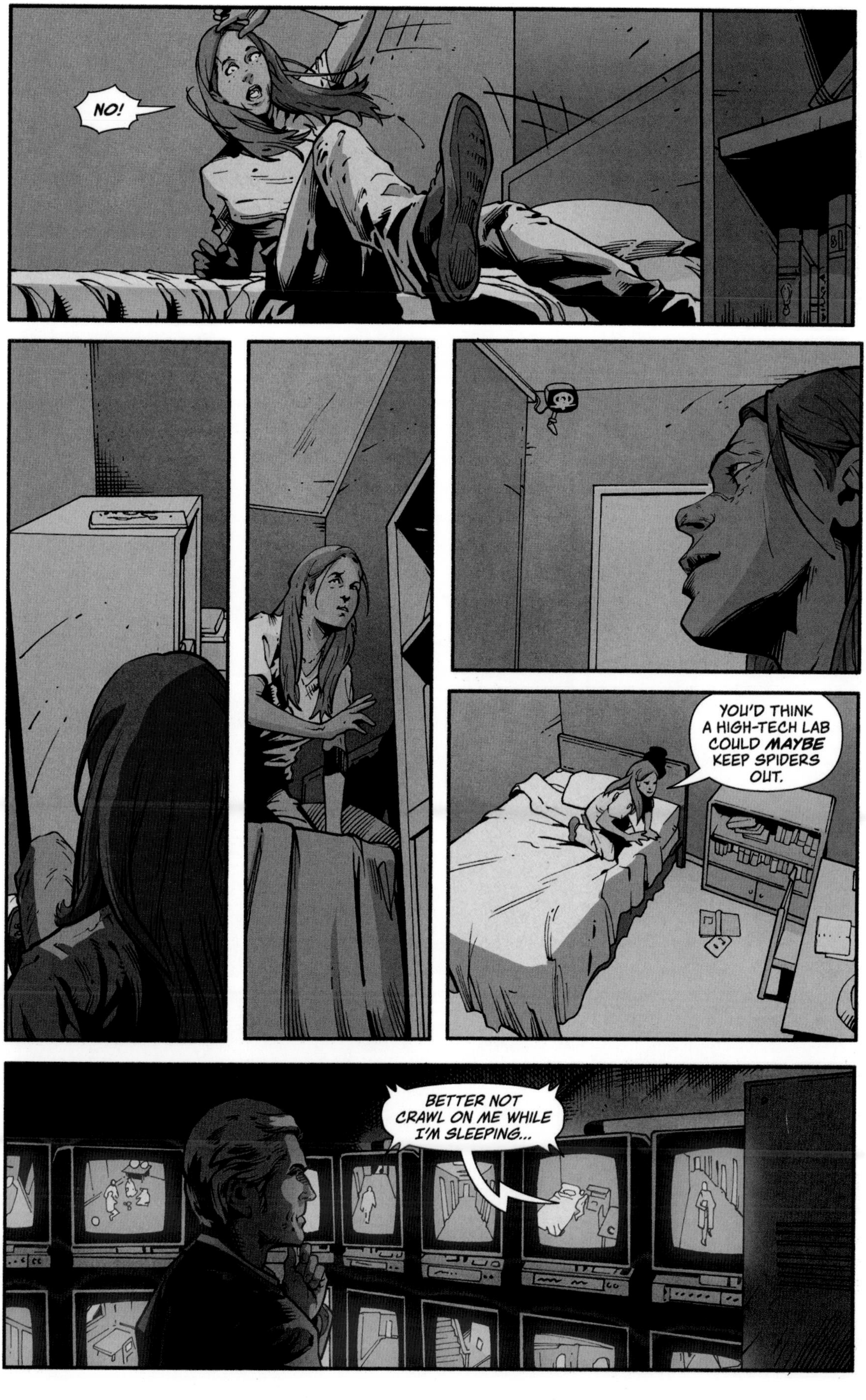
NO!
YOU'D THINK A HIGH-TECH LAB COULD MAYBE KEEP SPIDERS OUT.
BETTER NOT CRAWL ON ME WHILE I'M SLEEPING...

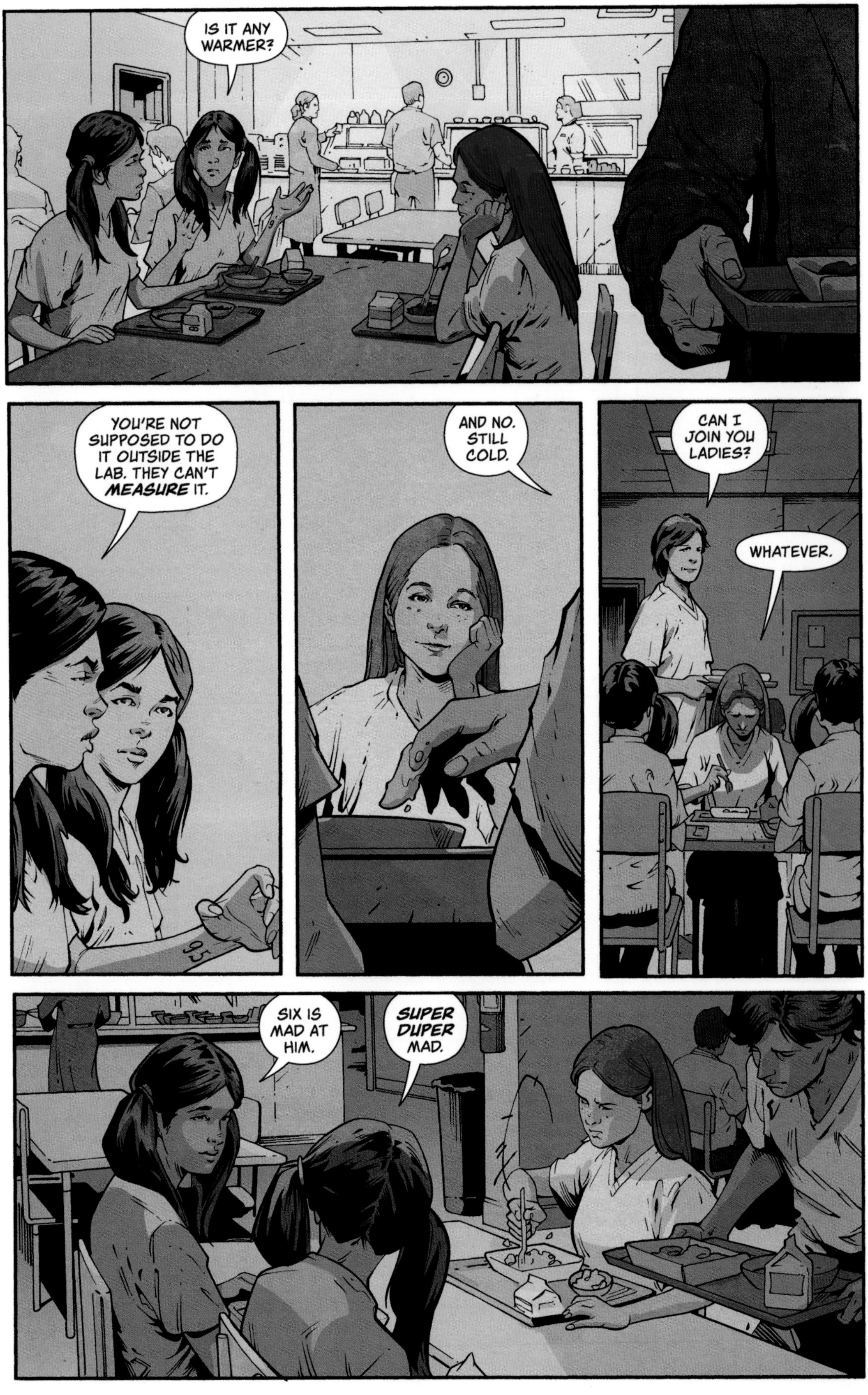
IS IT ANY WARMER?
YOU'RE NOT SUPPOSED TO DO IT OUTSIDE THE LAB. THEY CAN'T MEASURE IT.
AND NO. STILL COLD.
CAN I JOIN YOU LADIES?
WHATEVER.
SIX IS MAD AT HIM.
SUPER DUPER MAD.

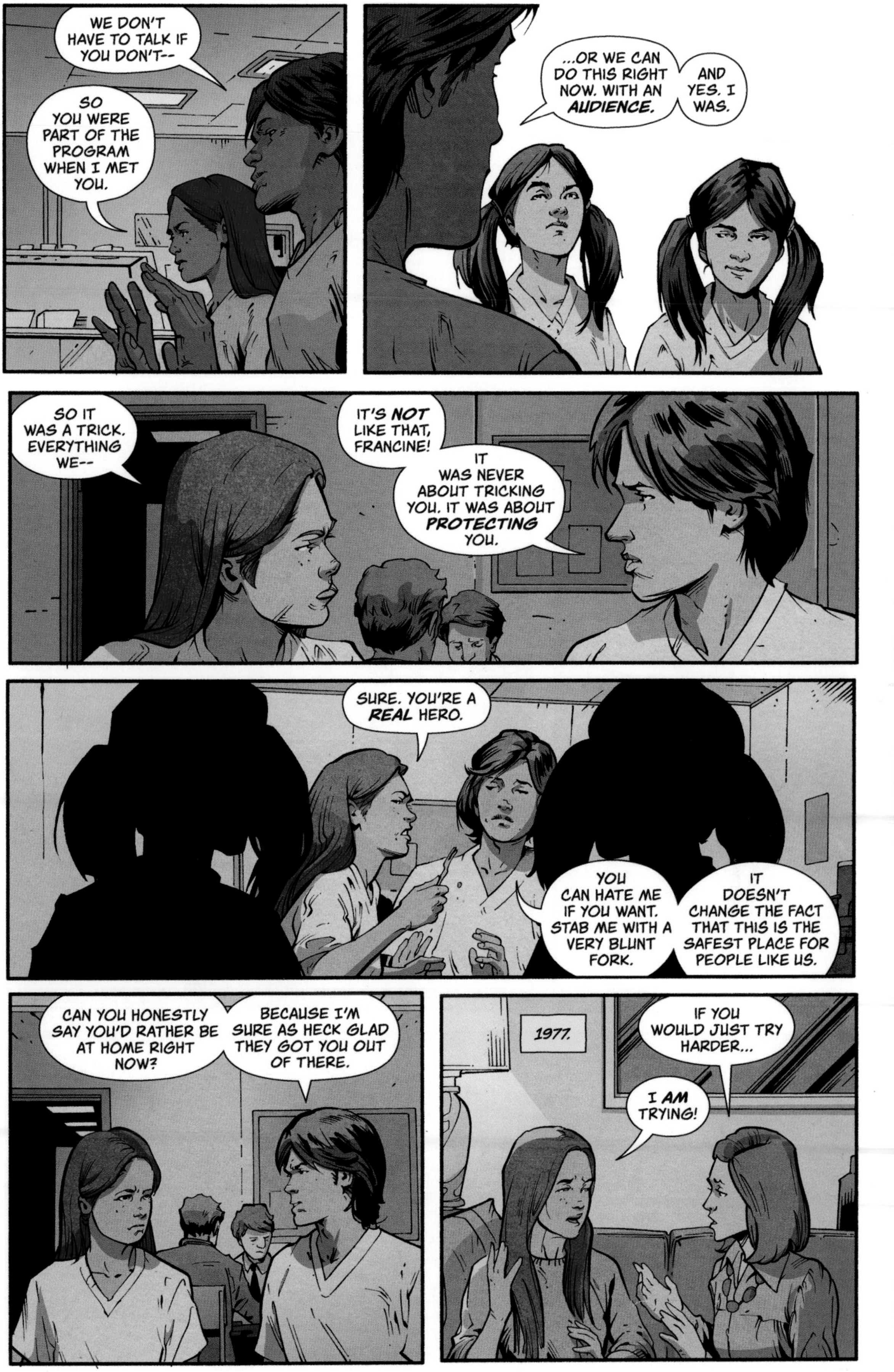

WE DON'T HAVE TO TALK IF YOU DON'T--
SO YOU WERE PART OF THE PROGRAM WHEN I MET YOU.
...OR WE CAN DO THIS RIGHT NOW. WITH AN *AUDIENCE.*
AND YES. I WAS.
SO IT WAS A TRICK. EVERYTHING WE--
IT'S *NOT* LIKE THAT, FRANCINE!
IT WAS NEVER ABOUT TRICKING YOU. IT WAS ABOUT *PROTECTING* YOU.
SURE. YOU'RE A *REAL* HERO.
YOU CAN HATE ME IF YOU WANT. STAB ME WITH A VERY BLUNT FORK.
IT DOESN'T CHANGE THE FACT THAT THIS IS THE SAFEST PLACE FOR PEOPLE LIKE US.
CAN YOU HONESTLY SAY YOU'D RATHER BE AT HOME RIGHT NOW?
BECAUSE I'M SURE AS HECK GLAD THEY GOT YOU OUT OF THERE.
1977.
IF YOU WOULD JUST TRY HARDER...
I *AM* TRYING!

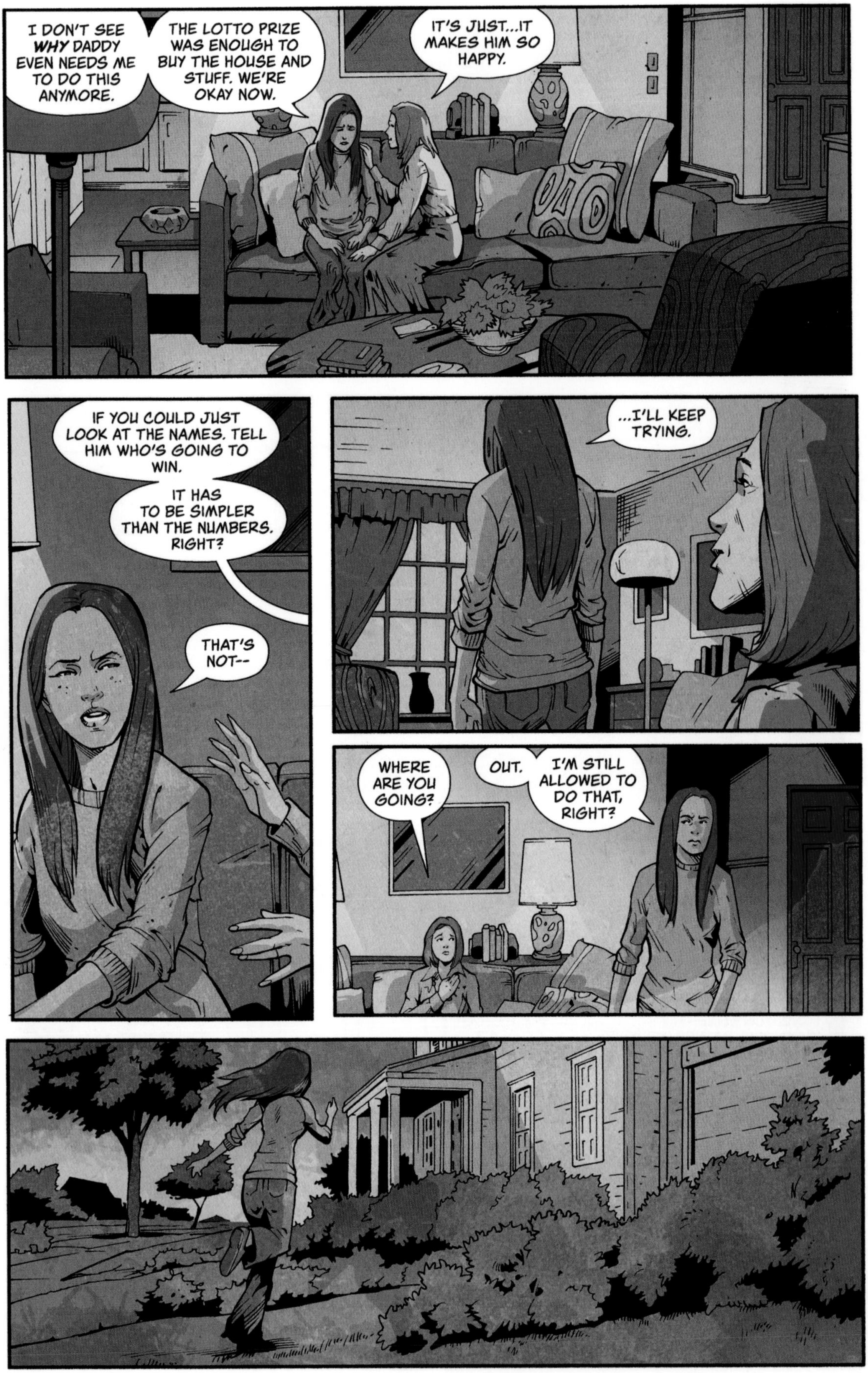
I DON'T SEE *WHY* DADDY EVEN NEEDS ME TO DO THIS ANYMORE.
THE LOTTO PRIZE WAS ENOUGH TO BUY THE HOUSE AND STUFF. WE'RE OKAY NOW.
IT'S JUST...IT MAKES HIM SO HAPPY.
IF YOU COULD JUST LOOK AT THE NAMES. TELL HIM WHO'S GOING TO WIN.
IT HAS TO BE SIMPLER THAN THE NUMBERS. RIGHT?
THAT'S NOT--
...I'LL KEEP TRYING.
WHERE ARE YOU GOING?
OUT.
I'M STILL ALLOWED TO DO THAT, RIGHT?

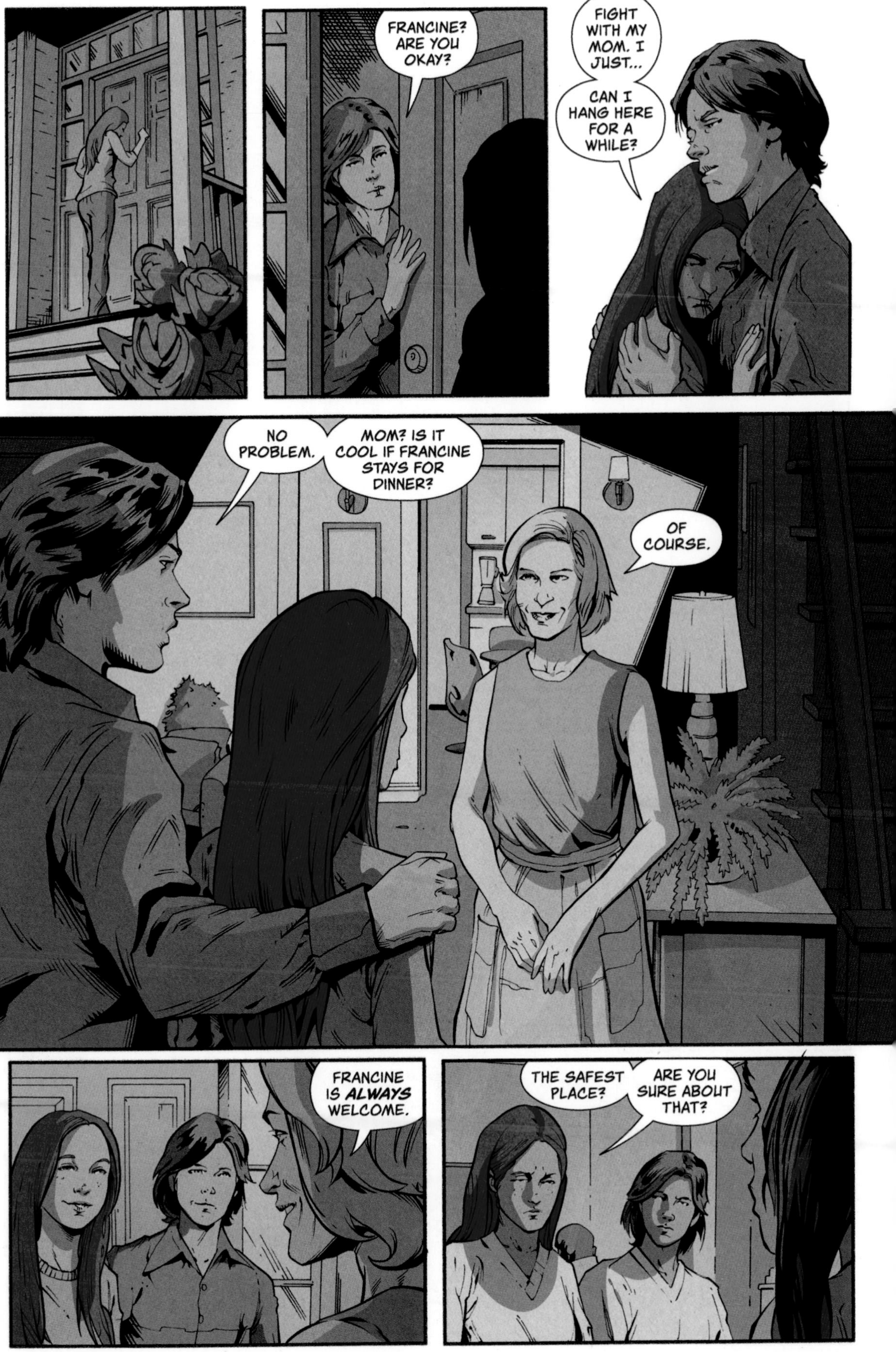
FRANCINE? ARE YOU OKAY?
FIGHT WITH MY MOM. I JUST...
CAN I HANG HERE FOR A WHILE?
NO PROBLEM.
MOM? IS IT COOL IF FRANCINE STAYS FOR DINNER?
OF COURSE.
FRANCINE IS *ALWAYS* WELCOME.
THE SAFEST PLACE?
ARE YOU SURE ABOUT THAT?

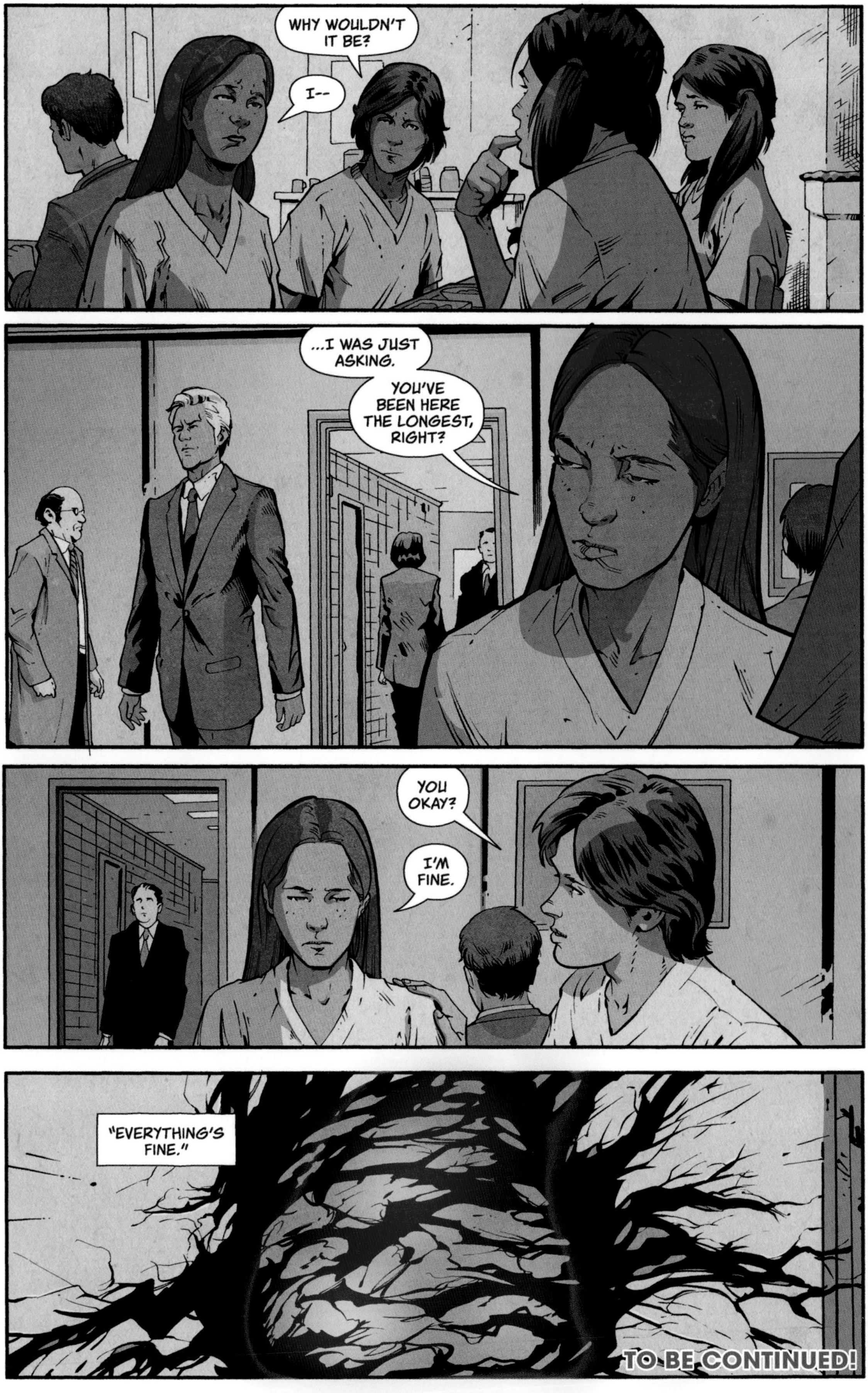
WHY WOULDN'T IT BE?
I--
...I WAS JUST ASKING.
YOU'VE BEEN HERE THE LONGEST, RIGHT?
YOU OKAY?
I'M FINE.
"EVERYTHING'S FINE."
TO BE CONTINUED!